WORLD of the WAZZLEWOODS

A Fern & Dale Fairy Tale

Tyrel Bramwell

Illustrated by
Edward Riojas

www.tyrelbramwell.com

This is a work of fiction. Names, characters, places, and incidents unless otherwise noted in the Author's Note either are the products of the author's imagination or are used fictitiously. Any resemblance to actual persons, living or dead, businesses, companies, events, or locales is entirely coincidental.

Cover art and interior illustrations by Edward Riojas, www.edriojasartist.com
Cover design by Tyrel Bramwell.

Printed in the United States of America.

ISBN-13: 978-1725140257
ISBN-10: 172514025X

Published in association with the Ferndale Chamber of Commerce.
PO Box 325
Ferndale, CA 95536
www.visitferndale.com

For children everywhere,
but especially in Ferndale

CONTENTS

Hi, there. My name is Fern. My brother, Dale, and I live with our parents and our dog Maggie at our Grandfather's house in the town of Cream City, California.

We haven't always lived here. We used to live somewhere much more normal. Seriously, ever since Mom and Dad brought us to live with Grandpa, we've been part of one unbelievable adventure after another.

It's because of Cream City's magic. That's right, I said magic. Cream City is a

small dairy town at the north end of California's Lost Coast. Some say the magic comes from the ancient Redwood trees that were used to make the old buildings. They're amazing trees that can live for two thousand years and grow to be hundreds of feet tall. My mom told us that they're the tallest trees in the world. Others say the magic comes from the fog that hovers over our town in the mornings. It doesn't really matter. My grandpa says it's better not to get caught up trying to explain away the magic but to just enjoy it's wonder.

And that's what Dale and I have agreed to do since we moved to Cream City. Grandpa lives in a big, old house, one made from the old Redwood trees I mentioned. It has lots of room for a family with two kids and a dog to move in. It's big and fancy with lots of what Grandpa calls gingerbread on it. Don't get confused. It's not actual gingerbread. Although, now that I mention it, I wouldn't be surprised if Cream City's magic could make that happen. Gingerbread is a fancy way of talking about the details on the old Victorian-style houses, it's like ornaments on a Christmas tree.

If the magic does come from the old Redwood, I think the reason there is so much magic here is because there are so many details on the old houses. Normal houses are basic, nothing magical about them, but Cream City houses are decorated and fancy, each little detail made out of old Redwood. Lots of magic!

But like I said, who knows if that's where the magic comes from. All I know is that it's real, and in my town when you look for it, you can see it. You'll understand what I mean after I tell you about how my brother and I first learned we lived somewhere special. We've had so many adventures that Grandpa suggested we write them down. "You'd hate to grow up, move away, and forget about the magic," he said.

I'm in charge of the actual writing, although so Dale wouldn't get upset, I agreed to let him write a story or two. He is also in charge of safe-keeping the stories, which, so that you know, we refer to as *fairy tales*. We haven't met an actual fairy, but if we ever do, it'll be in Cream City. I imagine they would be an awful lot like the wazzles, which is short for wazzlewoods, the species of Cream City creatures my grandpa created. They're how we learned about the magic. If you're ready, I'll tell you all about it.

We had just moved in. Mom and Dad were still unpacking boxes. Dale and I had been too, but were distracted by Grandpa's hobby. To pass the time, he whittled, which means he used a knife to make little sculptures out of wood. His house was full of them. The ones that caught our attention the most were no taller than a #2 pencil before it's ever been sharpened. They were little people, but not boring people. They were like the

house Grandpa lived in, covered in details.

When Grandpa caught us inspecting them, he said, "Aw, I see you found the wazzles."

"The what?" Dale said.

"The wazzles," Grandpa said.

"What's a wazzle?" I said.

"Not what. Who," Grandpa

said as he picked up the one Dale was staring at.

It was a tough looking little man with messy hair, no shirt, and a pair of pants that were shredded high above the ankles. He had on a backpack that looked like something an old time soldier might wear. Around his neck was a cowboy's bandana. All of this was carved out of wood and set apart by the colors and grains of the wood.

"Who's he, Grandpa? He's cool!" Dale said.

"This is Bareburl, but I think he lets his friends call him Barry."

Grandpa handed the wazzle to Dale, and Dale repeated his name.

"Why doesn't he have a shirt?" I asked.

Grandpa explained that each wazzle was carved according to the wood. It was the coloring and grain of the wood that determined what the figure would look like. As he spoke Dale and I inspected the other wazzles, noticing that, sure enough, wherever something changed, it was because the wood changed. Grandpa had used those changes to craft some very unique wazzles. The one on the very end of the shelf was holding a long sword with a blade that looked chipped from a thousand battles. But when I looked closer it was as Grandpa said, a jagged grain in the wood.

Now, imagine you're standing in a museum, looking at ancient treasures, but instead of grown-ups telling you not to touch, they hand them to you and let you play with them. Imagine a museum that is more like a toy store. That's what it's like at my Grandpa's. We were still getting used to that weird feeling when we saw the magic with our own eyes.

It was our dog that kicked it off. Ever since we arrived at Grandpa's house, she had been acting weird. One minute she was barking at the yard gnome like it was going to attack her, and then the next she was hiding under the living room coffee table with her paws over her eyes and refusing to obey our commands. That should have been our first clue that there was more to our new home than we knew. But it wasn't.

Instead, we learned about the magic when Maggie saw us holding wazzles. We didn't even notice she had walked into the room until she started one of her barking fits and then jumped up at Dale's hands.

Maggie is a little dog, about a foot tall and a foot and a half long. She used to be able to jump up and reach food in Dale's hands, but now that he has grown a few inches, she can't. Dale still panics every time she jumps for his hands. This time, he was so startled that he dropped Bareburl. That's when it happened. As the sculpture was falling to the ground, I saw it come to life. He went from a stiff sculpture to a moving, bending, twisting, turning person. No. He wasn't a person. He was a wazzle!

Bareburl did a summersault in mid-air, grabbed Maggie's fur, and pulled himself onto her back. She barked and tried her hardest to get him off. She twisted in circles as she snapped at him. It looked like a fur tornado hit Grandpa's living room. That's when it happened. That's when all the wazzles burst to life.

chapter

3

Maggie went round and round. A new
wazzle popped to life with every turn.
Each one joined the effort to stop our
wild dog from taking a bite out of
Bareburl. Dale joined the commotion.
Bent over, he chased Maggie through the
room. Wazzles sprang from the shelf and
bound off his back or slid down his arms
doing ninja-style flips toward the dog
and their friend. Bareburl didn't seem to
notice all the activity around him. He
pulled his bandana over his mouth,

raised one hand, and yelled, "Yee-haw!" like he was in the rodeo.

The last wazzle off the shelf was the soldier with the long jagged sword. His basic shape was the same as most wazzles, skinny except for a round stomach. This feature was usually unavoidable because of the wood Grandpa used for his creations. Burl wood. In case you're not familiar with the parts of trees and that sort of thing, burls are round growths on tree trunks and branches caused by some sort of stress during the growth of the tree. Dale thinks they come about when trees contain a high level of magic, at least when it comes to the ancient Redwoods.

Grandpa loves to carve his sculptures out of burls because the bumpy shape provides a unique pattern to the grain of the wood. Redwood trees are huge. When the old ones have burls they're also huge. Like as big as a small car. Grandpa doesn't use those big burls for wazzles. He uses little burls from branches. The straight part of the branch usually becomes the wazzles's legs or the neck and head. Most of the time the bulge of the burl becomes the belly of the wazzle, but sometimes it ends up being a head or one oddly large foot, a bubbly butt, or even something the wazzle is holding. Bareburl was rare that way. He didn't have a burl formation.

The soldier landed right in front of Maggie. He twirled his blade from side to side and then stabbed it into the floor. The sound caught Maggie's attention and

she stopped for a second to see what had happened. She tilted her head like dogs do when they're curious. The soldier made eye contact with her, and then she darted out of the room just as suddenly as she had stopped. Bareburl wasn't ready for her quick movement and tumbled back. He gripped her tail at the last moment and trailed behind her out of the room.

Bareburl spoke the first two words we ever heard from a wazzlc. The first was, "Yee-haw." The second was, "Help!"

chapter
4

When Maggie and Bareburl raced away, the room settled down. All the wazzles stopped right where they were.

Grandpa laughed and then said, "Really?"

The wazzles didn't move.

Grandpa moved across the room toward the doorway. He stepped over the wazzles like they were landmines and said, "You don't think my grandkids are stupid, do you? They saw the whole thing."

You would have thought the wazzles were so afraid to move that they were holding their breath. They're solid wood, so they don't breathe like humans, but on cue they all relaxed.

"Oh, Mr. Knife, we beg your pardon," said a wazzle with a top hat. "It's instinct, you understand? When the excitement ended, we realized you had guests in the house. We did the first thing that came to the ol' noggin." The wazzle lifted his hat and tapped on his head. It was a funny thing to see because the hat was most of the wazzle. If he was the height of a pencil, his actual body was no more than the bottom inch that you pinch between your fingers when you're writing. Everything else was top hat.

"No offense taken, dear friend," Grandpa said. "Please, let me introduce you to my grandchildren."

All the wazzles looked at us.

"This is Fern and her younger brother, Dale."

"Hi," I said with a wave.

Dale just stared at the wazzles. His mouth and eyes were wide open. He was speechless. The wazzle in the top hat stepped forward and said, "How do you do? I am Bogglestick Wazzlewood, Esquire, at your service." He took off his hat again and bowed toward me. When he stood back up I could see that he had on a little bowtie.

One by one the wazzles stepped forward. Bogglestick introduced them. "This is Ripplegrain Wazzlewood." A lady with long flowing hair that matched a long flowing dress curtsied. I could see why Grandpa carved her the way he did. Her wood twisted like a piece of licorice. Her hair and the length of her dress were covered in the added detail of a rippling grain.

Bogglestick continued, "And this is Garbleknot Wazzlewood." He had a giant forehead and a beard so long that it wrapped around his body several times before it was tied in a knot. It almost looked like a large belt buckle. He wore small rain boots. Real small. You might think Garbleknot's forehead was his burl because it was so big. It was big, but it wasn't the burl. Garbleknot was all burl with grains that swirled in all directions.

The soldier with the sword didn't wait for Bogglestick to make his introduction. He stepped forward and said, "I'm Jaggedbranch Wazzlewood, champion of the Wazzlewood Wars and sworn protector of the mystery of the magic."

Next we met Knickknack, Burlbump, Pizzlewizzle, Woodrough, Snapgrain, Crackburl, and many more.

After we met all the wazzles, we agreed that we should go find Maggie and Bareburl. We didn't fully understand the importance until Jaggedbranch stepped into the hallway and looked in the direction they had gone.

"We need to hurry," he said.

Something was wrong.

"What is it?" asked Garbleknot.

"The front door," answered Jaggedbranch. "It's open."

chapter 5

Everyone panicked at the news that the front door was open. Grandpa said to the wazzles, "You all know the dangers that await wazzles outside this house. Hurry. Bareburl needs you."

Dale and I didn't know exactly what Grandpa meant. "Why is it dangerous for wazzles to be outside the house?" Dale said.

Jaggedbranch answered. "Can you imagine being the smallest thing in the world? Can you imagine being somewhere where you feel safe, only to find out there is no security at all, but one threat after another waits to pounce on you, to swoop down and carry you off into the unknown, away from your home, away from your family?"

Dale and I nodded, and then Dale said, "Uh-huh."

Jaggedbranch was shocked. "You do?"

"Of course we do. We're kids," Dale said.

All the wazzles looked at Dale. Jaggedbranch said, "Oh, well, yeah, I guess you sort of do."

Garbleknot entered the conversation, "Your grandfather, Mr. Knife, keeps us safe in here. Outside we're threatened by the birds, cats, dogs, skunks, rats, and mice—"

He was cut off by Ripplegrain, "Not to mention the people."

"Oh, and rain and heavy winds. One big gust or downpour and he could be gone forever," added Pizzlewizzle.

Jaggedbranch frowned and said, "None of you have mentioned the greatest threat of all."

Dale said, "What's that?"

"The wayward wazzles," said Jaggedbranch.

"Who are they?" I said.

"Children," Grandpa interrupted, "there will be plenty of time to learn the history of the wazzles, but for now you must help them find Bareburl. Your parents have been outside at the moving truck. They'll be coming in soon with another load of boxes. You go and find Maggie."

Find Maggie. Grandpa didn't realize what he was saying. There was a reason we gave her that name. Have you ever heard of Ferdinand Magellan, the explorer? He was the first to sail around the earth. Maggie was named after Magellan because she loved to explore. She would follow scents and sounds anywhere. It took us forever to train her, because the slightest thing would catch her attention and off she would go, like a magnet pulled toward metal. Dad would joke that that's what she was really named after.

Jaggedbranch was still looking down the hall. He warned everyone that our parents were on their way back.

Ripplegrain tugged at my pant leg and said, "Pick me up, Fern."

Garbleknot did the same to Dale.

Ripplegrain said, "We'll go with Fern and Dale, everyone else should head to the zip line."

Our eyes lit up. "A zip line?" Dale said. "I want to go on the zip line."

Garbleknot laughed and said, "You're far too big, Dale. Trust me." He stood on Dale's shoulder.

The other wazzles rushed up stairs. We could hear their wooden feet scurrying across the floor. We looked at the ceiling and followed the sound.

Just then we heard Mom say, "Hey, kids." She and Dad had come inside. They were right in front of us. Ripplegrain was in my hands.

chapter 6

I was terrified that Mom and Dad would see Ripplegrain. They did.

"Oh, you've found Grandpa's wazzles," Mom said. "Which one is that?"

She grabbed Ripplegrain out of my hands. It was all I could do not to freak out, until I noticed that Ripplegrain had gone stiff. She was back to her sculpture form. I looked over at Dale to see if Garbleknot had done the same thing. He was gone!

Dale had on a baseball hat, and for a second I thought he had stuffed Garbleknot under it. Then I saw that the collar of his T-shirt was tight against his neck. He motioned over his shoulder with his head and eyes and smiled at Mom and Dad. He was nervous. Even though he didn't move, his shirt shifted and then shifted again.

Mom was looking at Ripplegrain. "She's called Ripplegrain," I said.

Dad chuckled. "Grandpa gives these guys the strangest names."

"He sure does," Dale said. He was scooting sideways around Dad.

Dad looked at him as if he was about to ask him what he was doing, so I spoke up, "Well, we were just heading outside. Is that okay?"

"Sure," Mom said.

Dad turned toward me. "Of course. Go explore your new town." He pulled his wallet out of his back pocket. "If you get to Main Street, make sure to go in the Golden Gait Mercantile. They have great old time candy." He handed me a few dollars. "That's for both you and your brother."

"Okay," I said. "Thanks."

Mom handed Ripplegrain back to me, and we dashed outside. We were standing at the bottom of the steps when I noticed Garbleknot dangling from the back of Dale's T-shirt. He climbed onto my brother's shoulder.

"Why didn't you go back to being a sculpture?" Dale asked.

Ripplegrain, who had come back to life, said, "He hates going stiff."

"It hurts," said Garbleknot.

"Really?" said Dale.

"Like you wouldn't believe," said Garbleknot.

"He's just being a big baby," said Ripplegrain.

I had turned and was looking at the house. "So where is the zip line?"

"There," said Garbleknot. He pointed at a powerline that extended from the top of Grandpa's house to the pole above the sidewalk. The wazzles were walking across it. Jaggedbranch led the way. He made it to the pole and then ran along the powerline in front of Grandpa's house. "Follow Jaggedbranch," Garbleknot said.

We ran under Jaggedbranch. As we did, Dale said, "I don't get why you call it a zip line." Garbleknot explained that once on the main line, a wazzle could easily slide down the wires connected to the houses.

The powerlines were a good way for the wazzles to travel through town. However, it was risky. Cream City has lots of birds and one of their favorite places to sit is on the power lines. Jaggedbranch, being the champion of the Wazzlewood Wars, insisted he go first for fear of the birds. It was a good thing he did.

Two houses down from Grandpa's a small group of blackbirds sat on the powerline. Jaggedbranch stopped when he noticed them, but it was too late. The birds saw the wazzles.

We were on the street below and couldn't get a close view of the birds, but I thought I saw something strange about them. They flew away from their perch, and that's when I thought I heard something strange about them.

"What kind of birds are those?" I said.

Ripplegrain said, "Blackbirds."

"Then what is that all over their bodies?" I said.

"Armor," said Garbleknot.

"They have armor?" Dale said.

"Of course they do" said Ripplegrain. "They're blackbirds."

She said this like it was a fact that all blackbirds have armor.

"We've never seen blackbirds wearing armor before," said Dale.

Ripplegrain explained that it was because of the magic. All blackbirds are dressed in full black armor. Even the blackbirds in your town are wearing armor. It doesn't matter where you live. It's a fact about blackbirds that you learn when you live in a town with magic.

Later, when Grandpa and Bogglestick filled us in on some of the history and details of what Grandpa called the magical world of the wazzlewoods, they told us that the magic allowed certain people to see the truth. The truth about blackbirds was that they wore a full suit

of armor. When a person with eyes that can see magic comes in contact with magic, he can see the truth. Everyone else just sees a blackbird.

You might wonder how a bird can fly wearing armor. That's what I wondered when I first heard all of this. I'm still trying to figure out the best way to describe just what kind of armor they have on. It looks like something a knight would wear, but it moves differently. It isn't so stiff. It's light and flexible so it can move with the bird. Maybe someday I'll be able to explain it better. Until then, it's just part of the wonder of the magic.

All of a sudden the birds flew off the powerline and attacked the wazzles. There were about six of them, and they came in fast. Jaggedbranch didn't wait for them. He jumped into the air with his sword. The first bird leaned back and flapped her wings together. She caught Jaggedbranch's sword, but his forward motion sent them both flying through the air.

The other birds dive-bombed the other wazzles. I thought I saw Bogglestick protecting himself with his top hat. It looked like he was swinging a funny looking baseball bat.

To my surprise, Woodrough did a back handspring that turned into several back flips. A bird was chasing him down the powerline. Woodrough stuck his foot out during the last backflip and kicked the blackbird in the beak.

Garbleknot yelled for Dale to run to the powerline pole in front of the next house. Something was hanging from the pole two thirds of the way up. It was Jaggedbranch, and he was about to fall.

When Jaggedbranch slammed into the bird, they both tumbled through the air. The bird let go of the wazzle's sword in order to use her wings and then flew back up to the powerline. Jaggedbranch, however, didn't have the advantage of wings. He continued to fall.

What he did have was his sword. So he stabbed it into the only thing nearby. The powerline pole. There he hung. He was an easy target.

The blackbird knew she had the upper hand. She swooped over to where he hung and pecked at him with her beak. It was all he could do to hold on to the sword with one hand and punch at the bird with the other.

Jaggedbranch's grip was slipping when Garbleknot noticed his fellow wazzle in danger. Dale delivered him to the pole in the nick of time. Garbleknot untied his beard and threw the end of it around the powerline pole. He caught it when it came around the other side. He held it like the reins of a horse, put his feet on the pole and leaned back. It was awesome to see. It was like he was a telephone repairman climbing the pole or a lumber jack climbing a tree with a rope wrapped around it.

A few flips of his beard and he was halfway to Jaggedbranch. Jaggedbranch let go of the sword. He couldn't help it.

He fell.

Thankfully, Garbleknot was there to catch him. Holding onto his beard with one hand, he grabbed Jaggedbranch with the other. The weight of the two wazzles pulled on Garbleknot's chin. Jaggedbranch clung to Garbleknot's back and the bearded tree-climber moved them up the pole to the powerline. Jaggedbranch grabbed his sword along the way.

What we saw next made Dale and me laugh out loud. Jaggedbranch grabbed the end of Garbleknot's beard and ran toward the other wazzles. Garbleknot stayed back until Jaggedbranch got as far away from him as the length of his beard would allow. Then Jaggedbranch motioned toward Garbleknot.

The wazzles are too small and they were too far away to tell for sure, but if I had to guess I would say Jaggedbranch gave Garbleknot a thumbs up, because as soon as he motioned, Garbleknot dove off the line and swung by his beard toward the other wazzles. He yelled the whole way. Dale thought it sounded like, "Hoorah!" I thought it sounded more like a long, "Ooo, Ow!"

Either way, their plan worked out great. Garbleknot swung right into the

middle of the battle. He
booted one bird
so hard that
it gave up
and flew
off. Still
holding
the end of
Garbleknot's
beard,
Jaggedbranch
charged the
blackbird that
had attacked him.
He swung his sword
with great speed. He struck the armor on
one wing and then the other. After three
or four blows it gave up and flew off, too.

The wazzles drove away all the blackbirds one by one. Garbleknot re-wrapped himself in his beard and tied it back into a knot in front of his stomach. Then he yelled down to Dale, Ripplegrain, and me, "Head to the park. We'll zip line down to you there."

"Okay," Dale said and then added, "That was awesome!"

"Yeah, we kicked those blackbird's butts, didn't we?" said Pizzlewizzle.

On our way to the park, we ran past a couple of blocks of old Victorian houses that looked like different colored versions of Grandpa's house. As we got closer, we passed an old red church. Ripplegrain paid close attention to her friends up above as we did. I noticed that she was afraid.

"What's wrong?" I asked.

She said, "There's an owl that lives in the Old Steeple."

After seeing how dangerous a blackbird could be, I understood the greater danger of an owl. I watched as the wazzles passed by the old church. I hoped they'd be okay.

The wazzles made it past the Old Steeple without a sign of the owl. I'm sure you know that owls don't like coming out during the day. They prefer it to be dark. If I would have thought of that at that moment, I would have told Ripplegrain so she wouldn't have been so scared for her friends.

The park was a block away and across a creek. It was the first time we had ever been there. The sign said it was called Firemen's Park. I remembered Mom had told us it was Cream City's only park. Apparently, all kinds of activities took place there. That's what she had said anyway. Somehow I don't think she meant activities that involved wazzles.

The wazzles on the powerline slid down a line that was connected to a nearby building. From there, they used the rain gutter to get to the ground.

"I don't see any sign of Maggie and Bareburl," I said as I looked around the park.

There was a baseball field in front of me and a playground behind it. Dale suggested we take a closer look at the playground. It was a good thing we did because that's where we found a clue that we were on the right track. It was at the bottom of the slide. Bareburl's backpack.

When we found it, Snapgrain became upset and started thinking about all kinds of bad things that could have happened to Bareburl.

"Why would his backpack have come off?" she said.

Ripplegrain tried to explain that it could have simply flew off as Bareburl tried to hang on to Maggie. She said, "It doesn't mean anything bad has happened to him. We should try not to think the worst. It doesn't do us any good to imagine bad things when we don't know if anything bad has happened."

I thought it was good advice. As I listened to Ripplegrain speak, it seemed to me that she was a wise wazzle. When I told Grandpa that I thought that, he agreed with me and said that she was very much like a mom to the other wazzles. He said, "To all of them except Garbleknot. To him she's more like a big sister."

I think we all must have been focused on Snapgrain and the backpack at that moment, because no one noticed that we had been surrounded. All of a sudden we heard a voice from the top of the slide. It sent chills through my body. Dale said it made him shiver with fear. It was the voice of Matchstick, the leader of the wayward wazzles.

chapter 10

Matchstick was a half a wazzle taller than normal. Grandpa had carved him with a trench coat and biker boots. His burl formed a hunch on his back.

Grandpa told me later that he had changed his name when he became the leader of the wayward wazzles. He used to be called Shimmerstick because his wood was naturally shiny, but when he went bad there was a fire that burned him. He looked like a long piece of charcoal now.

With a low, scary voice he said, "You really should be more careful when you come out into the wild." Then he grinned an evil grin.

When he spoke, the other wayward wazzles moved closer to us. The other wazzles, the good ones, I mean, gathered around my feet. Dale's, too. You might not think what I'm describing is very scary, so let me remind you that these creatures are about as tall as a rat is long and were scurrying at our feet just like rodents. It can get freaky fast. It would have been one thing if it was just a bunch of nice wazzles all around us, but the wayward wazzles looked wicked and gross and were getting closer and closer.

There was Matchstick, of course.

Treerot was a gray color. He looked like he was about to crumble into a thousand pieces. As for his shape, he was nothing but a hairy face. He hobbled along on his uncarved wood body. It gives me the creeps just thinking about it.

Then there was Barkbum. I'll give you one guess as to what he was named after.

Yep. His butt was bark. Every other part of his body was carved except for his rear end, which Grandpa left as bark. His pants hung low as if he was mooning the world. He had an attitude to match. One day Dale asked Grandpa what he was thinking when he carved him. Grandpa said he must have needed a good laugh that day and left it at that.

Splinters was a warrior. His hair was parted on the left side and slicked over. A sharp point stuck up in the back. He held a mace in his hand. If you don't know what a mace is, I'll tell you. It's a weapon from the time of castles and knights. It's a heavy ball with a bunch of spikes on it that hangs from a stick by a chain. You can imagine how it would hurt to get hit by such a thing. Splinters dangled the mace in front of him so that everyone could see that he meant business.

There were so many wayward wazzles that it would take me far too long to tell you about all of them. That said, you have to know about one more of them. The creepiest of the wayward wazzles. Hiveholder. Her burl was carved in the shape of a hornet's nest. She was wearing board shorts and a tank top. Her bare wood was covered in what looked like sting marks. When Hiveholder came to life her hive came to life, too. Don't ask me how. I have no idea, but a swarm of little wooden hornets hovered all around her as she moved closer to where we were at the base of the slide.

As she came closer, I whispered to Ripplegrain, "I'm allergic to hornets."

Dale heard me and said, "Even wazzlewood hornets?"

I shrugged my shoulders. I didn't want to find out.

chapter

11

What happened next happened very fast. Bogglestick started talking about peace and said something about the end of the Wazzlewood Wars. Matchstick laughed at Bogglestick and made fun of his top hat. That made Jaggedbranch squeeze the handle of his sword a little tighter, which made Barkbum bend over a little farther. More than that, it gave Dale an idea.

Hiveholder and her hornets were getting closer and closer, so Dale took off his baseball cap and tossed it at her. You should have seen it. He had perfect aim. The hat twirled in the air like a Frisbee and landed directly on top of her.

If Dale would have been listening better to what Bogglestick was saying, he might not have done that, because what Bogglestick had said was that at the end of the Wazzlewood Wars both the wazzles and the wayward wazzles agreed to live in peace. He also said that the group of wazzles that broke peace would not only have to face the other wazzle army, but also a stern punishment from the Fellowship of the Fog. He had been saying all of this in an effort to stop Matchstick from attacking. But it was

Dale, not Matchstick that broke the peace.

To be fair, even if Dale had been listening better, what he heard might not have stopped him from throwing his hat. After all, neither of us knew anything about the Wazzlewood Wars or the Fellowship of the Fog. Jaggedbranch gave us a very long and detailed run down of both, but I'll give you the short version for now.

The Wazzlewood Wars were started by Matchstick almost as soon as the last of the first wazzles came to life for the first time. There was a small number of them in the beginning. Matchstick got all but two to turn on Grandpa. Those two protected Grandpa but needed help.

They asked him to use his knife to whittle some more wazzles. That's why some of them are soldiers and have weapons while others don't. He made them that way to fight in the early battles of the Wazzlewood Wars. Anyway, not all of the new wazzles fought with the other two. Some of them joined Matchstick's army, and the wars continued for quite a long time.

The Fellowship of the Fog stepped in to bring about peace. Jaggedbranch explained that the Fellowship of the Fog is a gathering of chosen leaders from all the groups of creatures in and around Cream City. And there are a lot of them. The wazzles are the newest, but there are old, old, old groups. The oldest member of the Fog that I've met is Thrash. He's a bigfoot!

Like I said, everything happened fast. When my brother threw his hat over Hiveholder, Matchstick yelled, "Attack!" And boy did they. It was like a wooden river flooded our ankles. There were so many shades of wood.

Splinters of wood flew everywhere. Have you ever watched someone cut a piece of wood with a power saw? Do you remember all the saw dust that filled the air? It was like that.

Ripplegrain jumped down into the fight.

"Did you see where she went?" I yelled at Dale.

I had to yell. There is a lot of noise in war. Even if that war is a magical wooden one.

"No!" he said. "Can you see Garbleknot?"

"No." I said.

"I can't tell who's who." Dale said.

We both stared into the mass of wazzles, trying to find our new friends. It was like we had dumped out a bucket of LEGOs and were searching for certain pieces. We would see them and then when we looked a little closer, they were gone.

One thing we could tell by looking at the pile of wood at our feet was that the wayward wazzles were winning. There were a lot more of them. Hundreds of

them! I remember being
shocked at how many
I saw. I thought to
myself,
"Grandpa
whittled
all of
these?

That
must
be all he
does." It
was true. He
did
whittle
all of them. He
would just sit on his
front porch with his knife. He could carve

a wazzle in an afternoon and he had been making them for years.

Up until that point, Dale and I hadn't been touched. As I was looking for Ripplegrain and the others, I glanced toward Dale just in time to see two, three, four, then five, six, seven, and more and more wayward wazzles climb up Dale's legs. They climbed him like he was a tree. I screamed. They were at his shoulders. He was covered. I screamed again, but it wasn't because of what I saw. It was because of what I felt.

chapter 12

I screamed the first time because I saw the wayward wazzles climb all over Dale. I screamed the second time because they started climbing all over me. Dale was knocked down first. I went down right after. We both curled up into a ball for fear of what might happen to us.

I heard Dale say, "Leave my sister alone you rotten little wayward weasels."

A clown-like wayward wazzle with a stretched out neck and a burl for a head said, "Weasels? No. Wazzles," and then laughed a little *hee-hee* kind of laugh. When he stopped, he spoke something of a riddle.

"When a whittled wazzle is a wayward wazzle, the whittled wayward wazzle is a weasel not a wazzle. So while a whittled wayward wazzle can be a weasel, a weasel can never be a whittled wayward wazzle."

I don't know how long we were on the ground before we were saved. I know I started crying right away, and it felt like I had been crying for a long time. It couldn't have been too long though, because the wayward wazzles started to throw ropes over me, and they only got two across my shoulders when the arrival of our rescuers stopped them.

Remember how I told you that we had to cross a creek to get to the park? Our heroes charged up from that creek. They startled everyone with what you might call a battle cry. The wayward wazzles dropped the ropes and turned to see the source of sound. It was Maggie! She was barking. I could tell that she had been in the creek because as she barked, water dripped from her mouth.

I wish you could have actually been there to see it. She looked amazing. Bareburl was on her back, only this time everything was under control. She stood back on her hind legs like a horse, and Bareburl raised one hand as if to say, "Look at us. We're here to save the day."

If the wayward wazzles were thinking about attacking them, they didn't have a chance. Bareburl and Maggie charged. Maggie twisted and twirled. At each turn she sent a wayward wazzle flying to another side of the playground. Bareburl pulled on the nape of her neck and she jumped off the ground. When she landed, there were a few wayward wazzles under her feet. She licked them. They hated it.

I saw Jaggedbranch and Ripplegrain fight off Barkbum. Jaggedbranch grabbed ahold of Barkbum's belt. First, he yanked it up and then he pulled it tight. Ripplegrain said, "This is how you wear pants." She gave him a shove, and Jaggedbranch booted him in the rear.

Garbleknot was busy with Splinters who was about to swing his mace toward him. Before he ever had a chance, Maggie twisted in to him.

"Good to see you're okay, Barry," Garbleknot said to Bareburl.

"Why wouldn't I be?" was Bareburl's reply.

I noticed that Bareburl had a huge smile on his face. He was a fun-loving wazzle, to be sure.

Finally, all the wayward wazzles ran away. They scattered toward the houses and ducked under bushes, climbed drain pipes, or slid into the vents under the houses. I didn't see where Matchstick went, but I heard him as he left. He said, "You may have won the battle, but you broke the peace. Prepare for war!"

chapter 13

The wayward wazzles were all gone. Dale and I asked what Matchstick's threat of war meant for the wazzles. Bogglestick told us not to worry, but when he realized our concern wasn't going away he said, "We're not in the habit of leaving your grandfather's house and the wayward wazzles haven't stepped a foot inside it for years."

I was relieved, but Dale said, "You're just going to hide from them?"

Bogglestick answered, "It has been a good plan so far."

Jaggedbranch grunted and frowned and then said, "You saw how many of them there are. Each one is ruthless."

"But..." Dale started, but he didn't know what to say.

Just then Bareburl jumped down from Maggie's back. "I don't know about the rest of you, but my new friend and I are ready for another go-round." He smiled and then pulled off his bandana and wiped his brow as if he was sweating. Wazzles don't sweat. They're wood.

What happened next, took us by surprise. Dale nearly jumped out of his shoes, he was so stunned.

Maggie spoke!

I don't mean she barked. I mean she actually spoke words.

Her tongue was sticking out of her mouth. She had been panting from all the running and jumping. "I'd be happy to help," she said. Then she laid down at my

feet and started licking her paws like nothing new had happened.

Dale bounced from one foot to the other, pointed at her, and said "What?! You, you, you..." He was too excited to finish his sentence.

She kept right on licking her paws.

"You can speak, girl?" I said.

She looked up at me and said, "Of course, I can."

Bogglestick explained that those who have eyes to see Cream City's magic also have ears to hear it. When it comes to objects, like wazzlewood carvings, it brings them to life. He said, "There are a lot of artists who live in Cream City and the magic has been known to bring to life some pretty odd sculptures." He went on to teach us that when wazzles are not in their sculpture form, anyone who sees them, sees them walking and talking. Anybody could've seen the battle we just experienced. "But when it comes to animals," Bogglestick said, "The magic only lets certain people see and hear them as they really are."

Dale bent down by Maggie. "Say something! Anything," he said.

Maggie stopped licking her paws and said, "We should get some food. I'm starving."

Dale jumped back to his feet and did his sideways bouncing thing again. "Ha! She's starving!" he said. "She wants food!"

I was just as excited as my brother but somehow managed to control myself. I knelt down to pet Maggie. "I'm so glad we found you," I said. "Where'd you go?"

Maggie licked my face and said, "I'm not real sure. Eventually the creek."

Bareburl added, "Most of the time she was just trying to get me off her back. She was a wild one!" He turned to the other wazzles to make sure they would hear him. "But you know me. They don't call me Bareback Barry for nothing." He grinned.

Pizzlewizzle said, "No one calls you Bareback Barry."

Snapgrain added, "When have you ever ridden on the back of anything?"

If wazzles could blush, Bareburl would've. He shoved his hands in his pockets and kicked at the ground.

I think Ripplegrain felt sorry for him because she said, "There's a first time for everything. He did a fine job of riding Maggie." Everyone agreed and Bareburl smiled.

"That's right!" he said. "I'd like to see another wazzlewood give it a try."

Ripplegrain walked over to Maggie and me. She ran her hand through Maggie's fur. Bareburl joined her. She licked him. He fell backwards covered in slobber. Everyone laughed.

chapter 14

Maggie speaking pretty much marked the end of our first adventure in Cream City. We still had boxes to unpack. Already we had learned that our new home was in a magical town filled with wazzlcs and wayward wazzles that our grandpa had created, armored birds, and talking animals. Soon enough, Dale and I would find out that this was just the beginning of life in Cream City. When you live in a magical town, anything can happen. And let me tell you, it usually does.

As we left the park, we watched the wazzles climb their way to the top of a house and carefully scoot up a powerline to the main line that followed the side walk. Ripplegrain and Garbleknot stayed with Dale and me, and Bareburl rode on Maggie's back. Ripplegrain was a little nervous as we passed by the Old Steeple again, but this time I remembered that owls aren't very active during the day. I told her so. She replied with a soft smile.

The powerlines along our path were free of birds, and so we made it back to Grandpa's without any trouble. Mom and Dad had just gone into the house from the moving truck when we got home.

Grandpa was inside helping them unpack. He saw that Maggie was with us and let out a sigh of relief.

Ripplegrain, Garbleknot, and Bareburl had gone stiff so Mom and Dad wouldn't see them. Wazzles are kind of

fraidy-cats. I thought I heard a few wazzle footsteps upstairs. They hadn't come down yet.

"Hey, you're back!" Grandpa said and took the three wazzles from us and put them on the shelf.

Mom asked us what we thought of our new hometown. Dale and I looked at each other and said at the same time, "It's awesome!"

Dad had been in the other room, but he heard the question and our answer. He smiled and said, "I told you you'd like the Mercantile's candy selection."

"Oh," I said. "Sorry, Dad, we haven't made it to Main Street yet."

Mom asked where we had been. Dale told her Firemen's Park. Then Dad insisted we go spend the money he had given me for candy.

As we were going down the steps, Dad had moved over by Grandpa. Dale and I heard him say, "Where did all the wazzles go? There are only three on the shelf."

We turned to each other wondering how Grandpa would answer. He must've walked into another room or something, because we never heard what he said. After a few moments, we figured we could find out some other time. I had money in my pocket and candy to buy.

AUTHOR'S NOTE

Did you enjoy reading *The World of the Wazzlewoods*? Stories are fun, aren't they?

It's also fun to learn about the parts of the story that are true or based on real things. For instance, I have two kids and a dog. My daughter's name isn't Fern and my son's isn't Dale, but our dog's name is Maggie. A lot of what you read about Maggie is true. We really did name her after the explorer, Ferdinand Magellan, and like Fern and Dale's dad, I sometimes joke that we should have named her after a magnet. She really was hard to train. She can get very barky sometimes, and loves to jump and twirl around.

Another thing you might want to know is that Cream City, California is a real town at the northern most end of the Lost Coast. Its real name is Ferndale. It's a dairy town with lots of old Victorian houses just like Grandpa's. Fern and Dale were named after the town, so I had to think of something else to call it. Thankfully, back in the 1890s Ferndale became so well known for its butter that it used to be called Cream City.

When my family moved to Ferndale, we knew there was something magical about our new hometown. That's why I wrote this story. I wanted to share the magic with you as best I could.

This first adventure ended up in Firemen's Park because that's Ferndale's park, complete with a baseball field and playground. To get there from my house,

I have to walk under powerlines and pass by a lot of old Victorian houses. When I'm almost there, just before I cross the creek, I pass an old church now called The Old Steeple. It's been turned into a concert hall and is the home of Ferndale Music Company. And guess what? There is actually an owl that nests in the steeple. You can visit the Owl Cam website included below to get a view of the current owl family.

Fog truly hovers over Ferndale most days and we're surrounded by old groves of giant Redwood trees that have been alive for thousands of years and are hundreds and hundreds of feet tall. When I walk through the Redwoods, just like when I walk down Main Street, I feel like I'm living in a fairy tale.

If you walked down Main Street, you could do what Fern and Dale were about to do when the story ended. You could go buy candy at the Golden Gait Mercantile. It's an awesome old fashioned general store with all kinds of great candy. It was one of the first places my family visited when we moved to Ferndale.

The story is over, but that doesn't mean the fun has to stop. I saved the last pages of this book for you to draw your own wazzles. Don't forget to give them fun names.

Thanks for reading *The World of the Wazzlewoods*. If you liked the story, ask a grown-up to leave a review online.

Positive reviews help others learn about Fern and Dale's fairy tale. Who knows, maybe they have eyes to see and ears to hear the magic too.

Until next time,

About the Author

Tyrel Bramwell lives with his wife, two children, and their dog in the storybook town of Ferndale, California. In addition to being an author, he is the pastor of St. Mark's Evangelical Lutheran Church.

About the Illustrator

Edward Riojas is a masterful illustrator and fine artist. His work is found in sanctuaries, institutions, private collections and markets throughout the U.S. and across the globe.

You can learn more about the author, illustrator, and the real Cream City at the following websites:

- tyrelbramwell.com (author)
- edriojasartist.com (artist)
- visitferndale.com (Cream City)
- ferndalemusiccompany.com (owl cam)
- goldengaitmercantile.com (candy)

Draw Your Own Wazzlewood

Name: _____

Draw Your Own
Wayward Wazzle

Name: _____

68407314R00062

Made in the USA
Columbia, SC
09 August 2019